This book belongs to…

Upcoming books from The Hippocratic Press

Next in The Dr. Hippo Series: **"Peeper Has a Fever"** is a story about a little frog who loves to hop and dive but who develops a fever... Also coming are stories about a giraffe with a sore throat, a polar bear with a cold, and a moose with loose poops (vomiting and diarrhea.) Watch for them all!

Ordering information

Order books from your local book retailer, your online book source, or directly from:

The Hippocratic Press
281A Fairhaven Hill Road
Concord, MA 01742
www.hippocraticpress.com

The Little Elephant with the Big Earache

by Charlotte Cowan, M.D. *illustrated by* Elaine Garvin

book design by Labor Day Creative

The Hippocratic Press
Concord, MA

Dedicated to the physicians and staff at the MassGeneral Hospital *for* Children in appreciation of their training, expertise and compassion in the care of sick children. —*C.C.*

Dedicated to my granddaughters, Ellie and Tilda. —*With Love, E.G.*

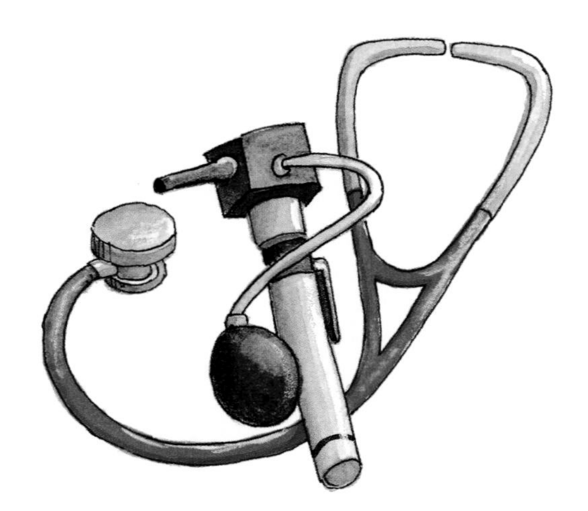

The purpose of this book is to educate. While every effort has been made to ensure its accuracy, its content should not be construed as definitive medical advice and is not a substitute for the professional judgment of your child's health care provider in diagnosing and treating illness. Because each child's health care needs are unique and because medical knowledge is always evolving, please consult a qualified health care professional to obtain the most current recommendations appropriate to your child's medical care. Neither the author nor the publisher shall be liable for any outcome or damages resulting from reliance upon the content of this publication.

First American edition 2004 published by The Hippocratic Press.

Charlotte Cowan, M.D. and Elaine Garvin assert the right to be identified as the author and the illustrator of this work.

Printed in China.

Library of Congress Control Number: 2004105489

ISBN 0-9753516-0-5

The little elephants arrived on Wednesday. They rushed down to the river to find their cousin Eddie.

"We're here," they shouted, "we're here for your birthday!"

Before long Eddie said, "Sam, I have an idea!"

Sam smiled: "That will be perfect for your party. We'll surprise everyone and win the Mud Castle Contest for sure!"

Eddie added: "I can't wait until Saturday! We'll have the contest—and cake and ice cream, too!"

Their secret sculpture wasn't quite finished when they heard Eddie's Mom calling: "It's time for dinner! Squirt yourselves off, please!"

"Okay, Mom, we're coming," yelled Eddie.

Not long after dinner, the little elephants were ready for bed. "Mom," said Eddie, "please read us a story."

"Of course," she replied, "but then you must go straight to sleep."

The stars were still twinkling when Eddie woke up. "My ear hurts," he thought. "I need to find my Mom."

The little elephant nudged his mother.
"Eddie," she asked, "what's wrong?"

He began to cry.

"Little one," she said, climbing out
of bed, "let's go into the kitchen."

"Sweet peanut," said his mother, "you've had a cold and may have an ear infection now. Let's take your temperature and give you something to make you feel better tonight. We'll visit Dr. Hippocrates in the morning."

"Will this make me *all* better, Mom?"

"It will make you feel *much* better, Eddie. Tomorrow, we'll see if Dr. Hippo thinks you need another medicine, too."

"I hate this," he complained, but Eddie swallowed every drop.

"Great job! Have some juice and then we'll go sit on the porch."

Eddie leaned against his mother and watched the stars. Soon his eyes began to close. "I'm okay now, Mom," he said. His mother rocked and rocked.

"Don't worry little one," she said quietly, "Dr. Hippo will help us soon."

Eddie's Mom called the doctor right after breakfast and, before long, they stood at Dr. Hippo's door.

Eddie began to feel nervous. "I want to go home," he whispered.

RHINO'S
RESTAURANT

While they waited, Eddie watched the giraffes outside.
"Hey Mom, what do giraffes have on *their* birthdays?" he asked.

"Maybe they have chocolate cake," she answered, smiling.

Dr. Hippo appeared. "Hello Squirt," he said. "I understand that you've had a bad night."

His mother explained, "Eddie has an earache."

"And my cousins are here for my birthday!" he added.

Dr. Hippo smiled. "Your *birthday!* Well, we certainly need to get you better!"

Dr. Hippo asked lots of questions and then said, "Eddie, I'll listen to your heart and lungs and then I'll look in your mouth and ears."

"You have a good heart, Eddie."
"Pretend to blow out birthday candles."
"Pant like a puppy dog, please!"

When it was time to check Eddie's ears, Dr. Hippo said, "I always begin with the ear that *doesn't* hurt."

First he peeked inside with his flashlight; then he used a little balloon to blow air inside the ear.

"That tickles," said Eddie.

Dr. Hippo smiled: "I don't see any butterflies today. Let's see the other ear."

Eddie hesitated. "But that one hurts," he said. His mother helped him turn his head.

"Dr. Hippo will be very gentle," she promised.

"Uh-oh," he said. "This eardrum looks sore. No wonder you had trouble sleeping last night, Eddie!"

Dr. Hippo continued: "Eddie has an early ear infection that might go away by itself. Let's watch him carefully off of antibiotics, making sure that he stays comfortable."

Eddie was getting his blanket.

"If his fever continues or increases, or if he feels worse, *please* come back to see me."

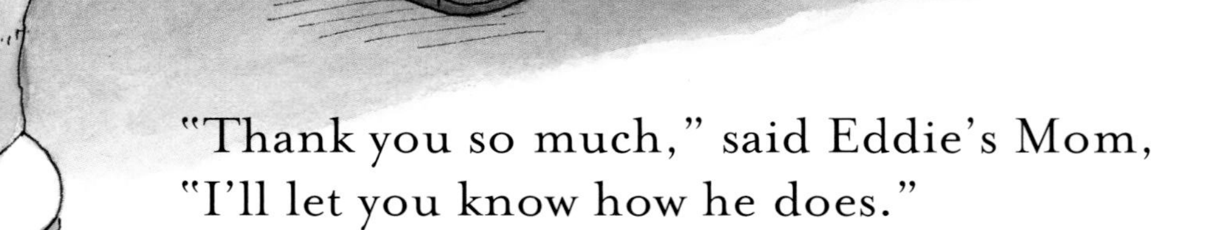

"Thank you so much," said Eddie's Mom, "I'll let you know how he does."

Then Dr. Hippo said, "Goodbye for now. I hope you feel better soon, birthday boy!"

The next day, Eddie stayed at home. While his cousins went down to the river, he rested and baked a cake with his Mom. "Are you well enough to lick the spoon?" she asked.

"Yes," smiled Eddie. "I feel much better!"

Saturday was Eddie's party!

"Run down and finish your castles," suggested Eddie's Mom, "and then we'll have cake and ice cream."

Before long, it was time for the judges to choose the *best* mud castle.

JUDGE
JUDGE
ICE CREAM
SALSA

Eddie blew out his candles and then they announced the contest winner. "All of the castles are wonderful," said the judges, "but the blue ribbon goes to Eddie and Sam for their surprise: they made an *elephant!*"

The cousins trumpeted with excitement and hurried to the river for a closer look. "Wow! Look at that!" they shouted.

Eddie's mother smiled. "Does your elephant have an earache?" she asked.

"No, Mom," laughed Eddie, "our elephant is fine—and so am I!"

THE END